ABRAMS BOOKS FOR YOUNG READERS
NEW YORK —

NINETY-THREE
IN MY FAMILY

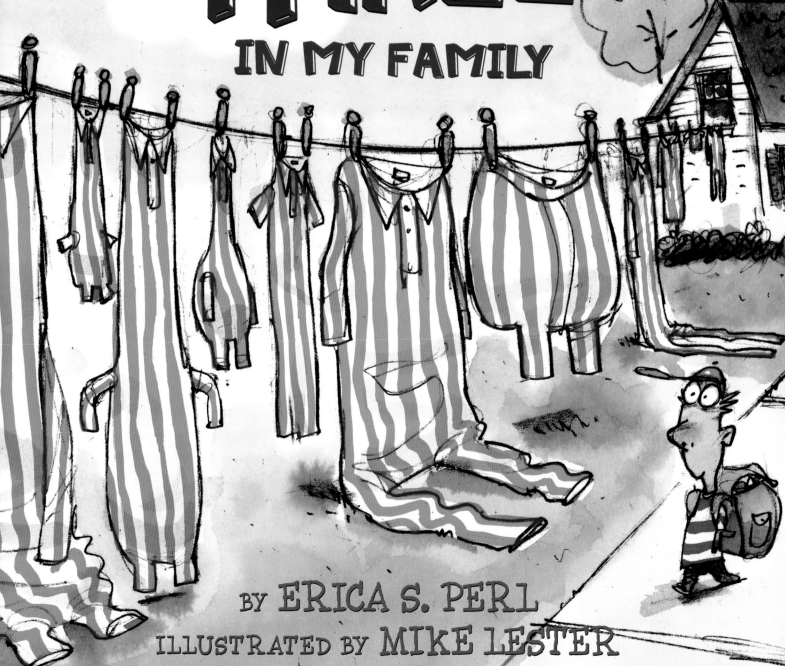

BY ERICA S. PERL

ILLUSTRATED BY MIKE LESTER

One day, my teacher asked me,
"How many live with you?"
I counted quickly in my head.
I told her, "Ninety-two."

She laughed. "You must be joking!
However can that be?"

I shrugged my shoulders and began
To list my family:

There's twenty-seven owls,
Ten cats, eleven dogs,
A pygmy hippo named Bernice,
And eight blue speckled frogs.

My mommy and my daddy,
My sister's gerbil, Ed,
Six goldfish and my sisters,
Darlene and Winifred.

Whenever people ask me
How many live with me,
I tell them true, there's ninety-two.
Plus one (that's me!), we're ninety-three.

Sometimes we order pizza
To feed our family.
We tell them, "Make it extra big,
To feed all ninety-three."

The frogs like pepperoni.
The owls like theirs plain.
The tigers leave their pizza crusts.
Who eats them? Our Great Dane.

Bernice, she likes her pizza cold,
And so does our red fox.
Then when we've eaten all the food,
Our goat, he eats the box.

There's twenty-seven owls,
Four lions, and a duck.
At my house, if you don't eat fast
You'll find you're out of luck!

My mommy and my daddy,
That hungry gerbil, Ed,
Six goldfish, and my sisters,
Darlene and Winifred.

Whenever people ask me
How many eat with me,
I tell them true, there's ninety-two.
With me, you see, we're ninety-three.

I'll tell you, it gets crowded
When we get in the car.
And Mom and Dad get cranky
If we have to drive too far.

The lions tease the tigers.
The penguin wants to drive.
The armadillos all insist
They must be home by five.

The pink flamingos like to stick
Their heads out in the breeze.
The squirrel sits on Daddy's head
(Which always makes him sneeze.)

There's twenty-seven owls,
All squeezed in the backseat.
And where's that growling coming from?
Right there! The bear beneath my feet!

My mommy and my daddy,
That carsick gerbil, Ed,
Six goldfish, and my sisters,
Darlene and Winifred.

Whenever people ask me
How many ride with me,
I tell them true, there's ninety-two.
Including me, we're ninety-three.

But when we get back home again,
We get along just great.
I help my sisters wash the pets.
That's right, all eighty-eight!

We have to watch them closely.
(Some like to drink shampoo.)
And if one gets a bubble bath,
The others want one, too.

When all are finished bathing,
We dry the pets with towels.
My sisters mop the bathroom floor
While I blow-dry the owls.

And when it is our bedtime,
We never make a fuss.
Instead, we snuggle and read books—
All ninety-three of us.

There's twenty-seven owls,
Five gophers and two llamas.
And all of us, except Bernice,
Wear matching striped pajamas.

My mommy and my daddy,
That sleepy gerbil, Ed,
Six goldfish, and my sisters,
Darlene and Winifred.

Whenever people ask me
How many sleep with me,
I tell them true, there's ninety-two.
And then there's me, so ninety-three.

So, though it's often hectic,
My life's never a bore.
"That's good," I told my teacher,
"Because . . .

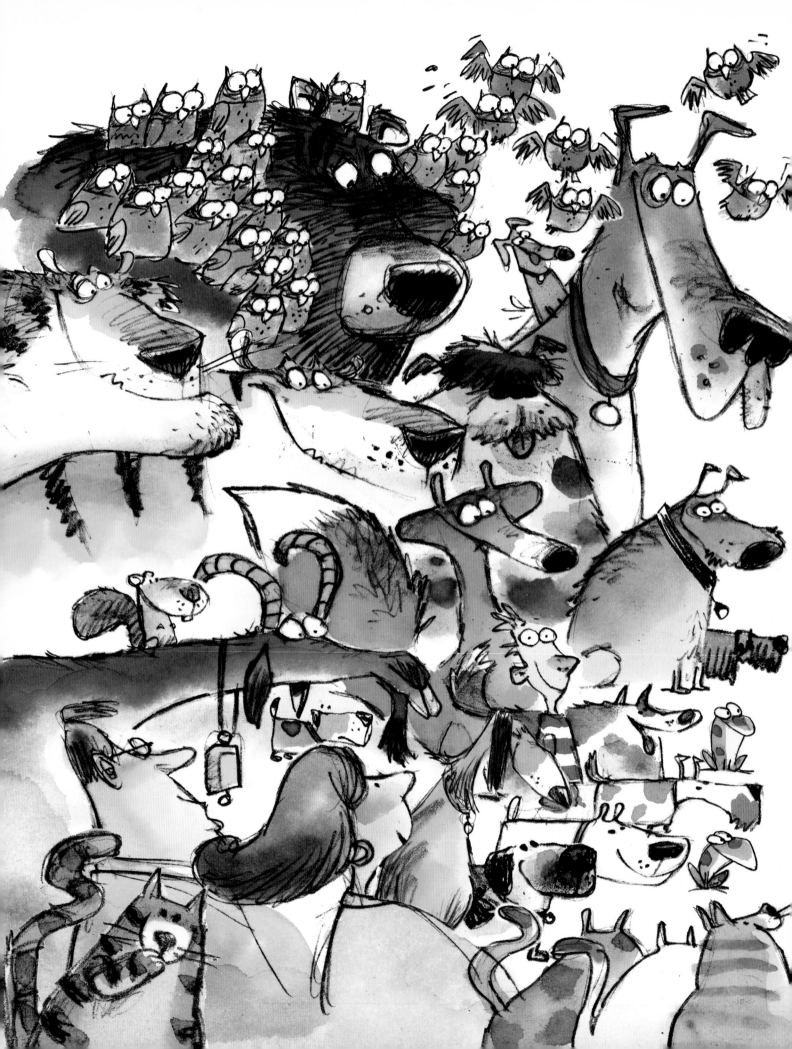

... we'll soon be ninety-four!"

Tally:

27 owls
10 cats
11 dogs
1 pygmy hippo
8 frogs
1 gerbil
6 goldfish
1 fox
1 goat
4 lions
1 duck
2 tigers
1 penguin
3 armadillos
2 flamingos
1 squirrel
1 bear
5 gophers
2 llamas
_____

88 animals

(plus 2 parents
2 sisters
1 brother—that's me)
93 total in family

(plus baby pygmy hippo = 94)

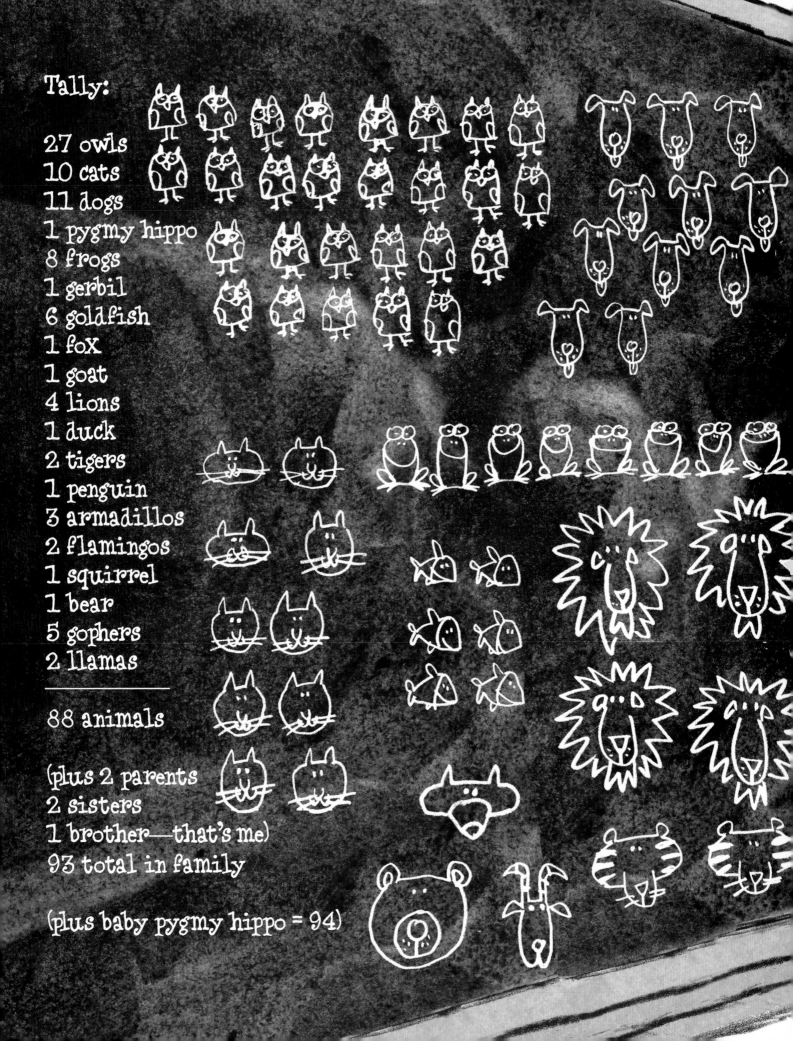

To my parents
—E.S.P.

To the children of Iraq,
may you be free to laugh.
—M.L.

AUTHOR'S ACKNOWLEDGMENTS
Thank you, as always, to Mike, Franny, and Bougie, for being my wonderful home team.
Thanks also to Susan Van Metre, Jason Wells, George Bates, and Mike Lester, for your talent,
your dedication, and (in the case of Mike L.) your armadillos.

ARTIST'S NOTE
The pictures in this book were drawn with pen and ink, scanned into a computer,
and digitally colored.

Designer: Vivian Cheng
Production Manager: Alexis Mentor

Library of Congress Cataloging-in-Publication Data:
Perl, Erica S.
Ninety-three in my family / by Erica S. Perl ; illustrated by Mike Lester.
p. cm.
Summary: A young boy explains to the mailman that his family consists of ninety-three members,
including his parents, sisters, and an assortment of pets.
[1. Counting—Fiction. 2. Family—Fiction. 3. Pets—Fiction. 4. Animals—Fiction. 5. Stories in rhyme.]
I. Title: 93 in my family. II. Lester, Mike, ill. III. Title.
ISBN 10: 0-8109-5760-4
ISBN 13: 978-0-8109-5760-2
PZ8.3.P4225Nin 2006
[E]—dc22
2005032394

Printed and bound in China
10 9 8 7 6 5 4 3 2 1

HNA
harry n. abrams, inc.
a subsidiary of La Martinière Groupe
115 West 18th Street
New York, NY 10011
www.hnabooks.com